The Adventures of
CHUPACABRA CHARLIE

Written by Frederick Luis Aldama
Illustrated by Chris Escobar

Mad Creek Books, an imprint of
The Ohio State University Press
Columbus

Library of Congress Cataloging-in-Publication Data
Names: Aldama, Frederick Luis, 1969– author. | Escobar, Chris, illustrator.
Title: The adventures of Chupacabra Charlie / written by Frederick Luis Aldama ; illustrated by Chris
    Escobar.
Description: Columbus : Mad Creek Books, an imprint of The Ohio State University Press, [2020] |
    Audience: 4–10. | Audience: 2–3. | Summary: As the weather changes and food becomes scarce in
    Mexico, a young monster and a human girl who live on the Mexico/United States border embark
    on an adventure to free children kept in cages on the other side of The Wall.
Identifiers: LCCN 2019045462 | ISBN 9780814255865 (paperback) | ISBN 0814255868 (paperback)
    | ISBN 9780814277935 (ebook) | ISBN 0814277934 (ebook)
Subjects: CYAC: Chupacabras—Fiction. | Mexican-American Border Region—Fiction. | Hispanic
    Americans—Fiction. | Adventure and adventurers—Fiction.
Classification: LCC PZ7.1.A42 Ad 2020 | DDC [E]—dc23
LC record available at https://lccn.loc.gov/2019045462

Cover design by Lindsay Starr
Type set in Palatino
Printed by Pacom

PRINTED IN THE REPUBLIC OF KOREA

∞ The paper used in this publication meets the minimum requirements of the American National
Standard for Information Sciences—Permanence of Paper for Printed Library Materials. ANSI Z39.48-1992.

To all our niños who dare
to dream larger than life.

My name's Charlie. I'm a Chupacabra. One of those creatures from made-up human stories. A monster. Except I'm the real deal.

I live with my Mamá Lula and Papá Rolo. We live above the Humans in a *cuarto de azotea*.

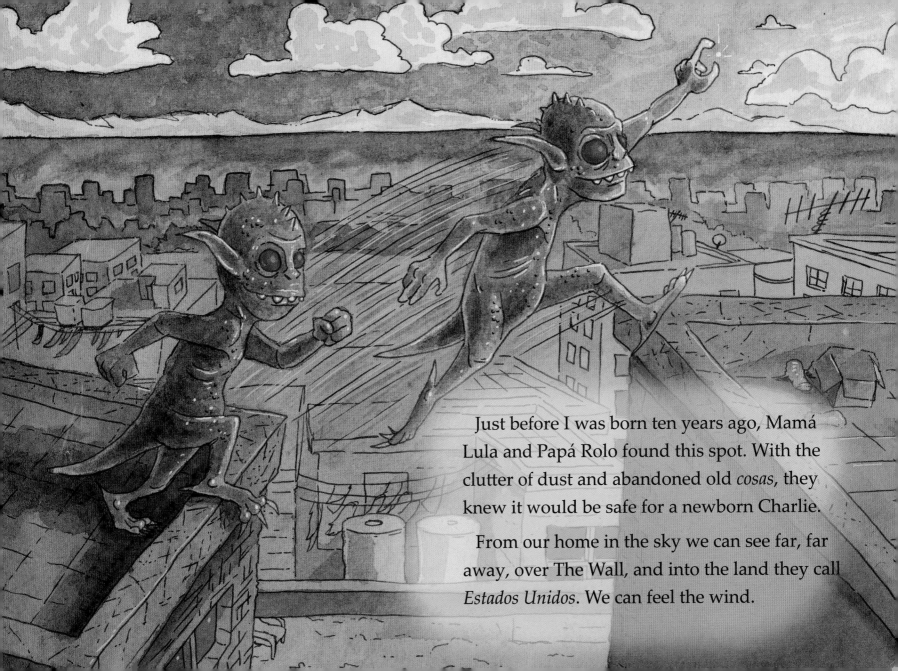

Just before I was born ten years ago, Mamá Lula and Papá Rolo found this spot. With the clutter of dust and abandoned old *cosas*, they knew it would be safe for a newborn Charlie.

From our home in the sky we can see far, far away, over The Wall, and into the land they call *Estados Unidos*. We can feel the wind.

I wake, wipe the sleep from my eyes, take a quick shower, and then sit for my *desayuno*. With Papá Rolo, all those left-behind *cosas* come alive: the chalkboard with words and numbers. *Libros* open to magical adventures in other lands.

During meals, Mamá Lula and Papá Rolo talk about the old days, before the weather changed and the food ran out. Papá Rolo talks about growing up in Chihuahua with his 12 siblings. Mamá Lula tells stories about the days when she swam in Great Big Blue with *tortugas* and shimmery blue *atúnes*.

Smiles turn to frowns as they talk about how the sea life disappeared and the corn dried up on the land. How Humans became angry and no longer wanted to be our friends. To find food, Mamá Lula and Papá Rolo moved to the city and began dumpster-diving for scraps of food.

We constantly work on what Mamá Lula and Papá Rolo call "etiquette." They don't want me to turn out like my *primos* who sit bent over, hop like kangaroos, and love to taunt and tease other *animalitos*. It's no wonder, they say, that the Humans tell wild and frightening stories about us.

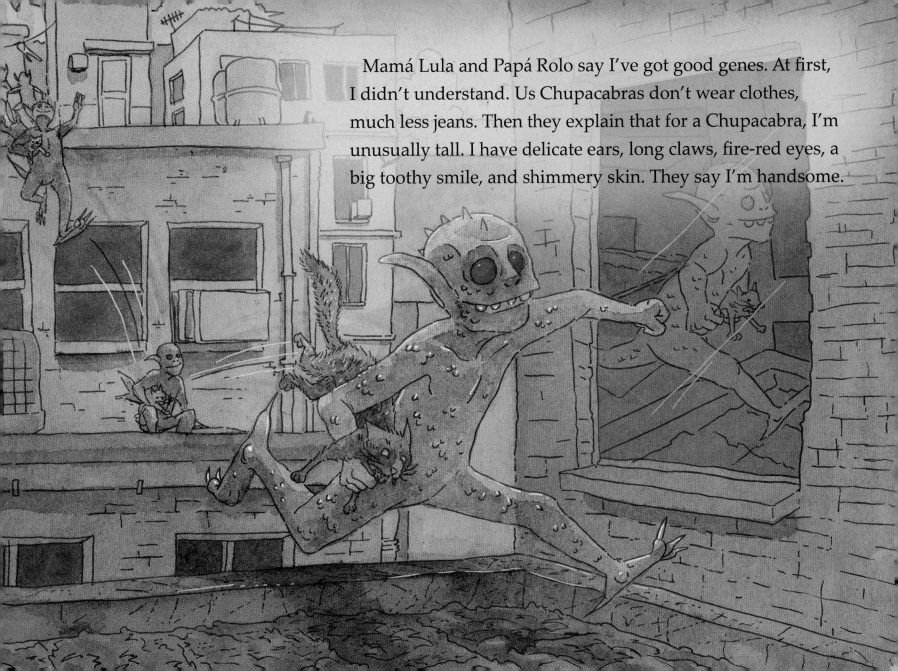

Mamá Lula and Papá Rolo say I've got good genes. At first, I didn't understand. Us Chupacabras don't wear clothes, much less jeans. Then they explain that for a Chupacabra, I'm unusually tall. I have delicate ears, long claws, fire-red eyes, a big toothy smile, and shimmery skin. They say I'm handsome.

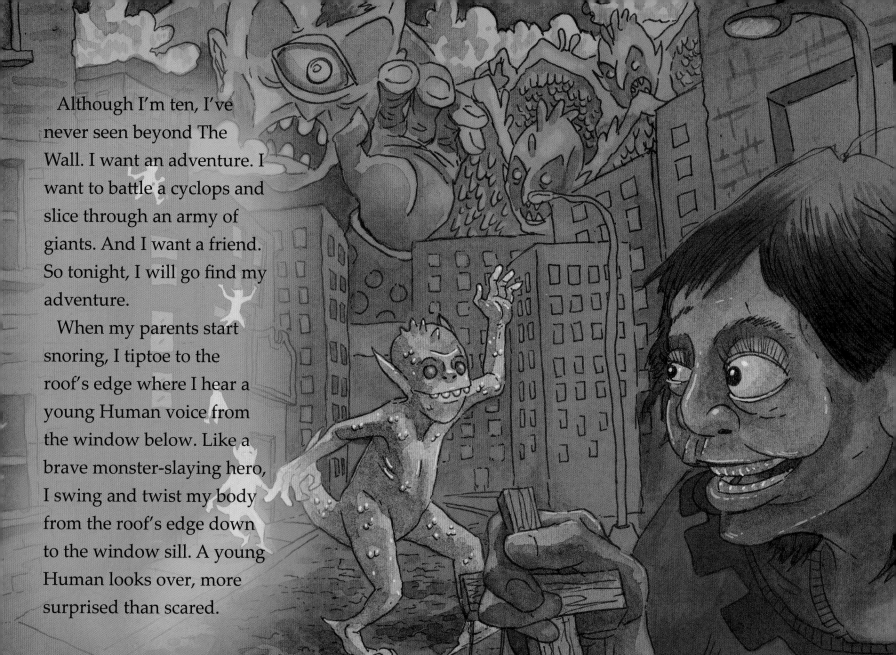

Although I'm ten, I've never seen beyond The Wall. I want an adventure. I want to battle a cyclops and slice through an army of giants. And I want a friend. So tonight, I will go find my adventure.

When my parents start snoring, I tiptoe to the roof's edge where I hear a young Human voice from the window below. Like a brave monster-slaying hero, I swing and twist my body from the roof's edge down to the window sill. A young Human looks over, more surprised than scared.

"Hi. I'm Charlie. I live upstairs. *¿Cómo te llamas?*" I ask in my best Spanish.

"I'm Lupe."

"Did you just move here?"

"Yeah."

She hands me a puppet. We smile at each other.

"Do you like adventures?"

"What kind of adventures?"

"C'mon, I'll show you!"

It's late now, and our families are fast asleep. Lupe and I grab a shoulder sling bag and fill it with leftover bacon quesadillas and a couple of cans of *Jumex*. She grabs her skateboard. I grab my kick scooter. We race down the shadowy hallways as we make our great escape.

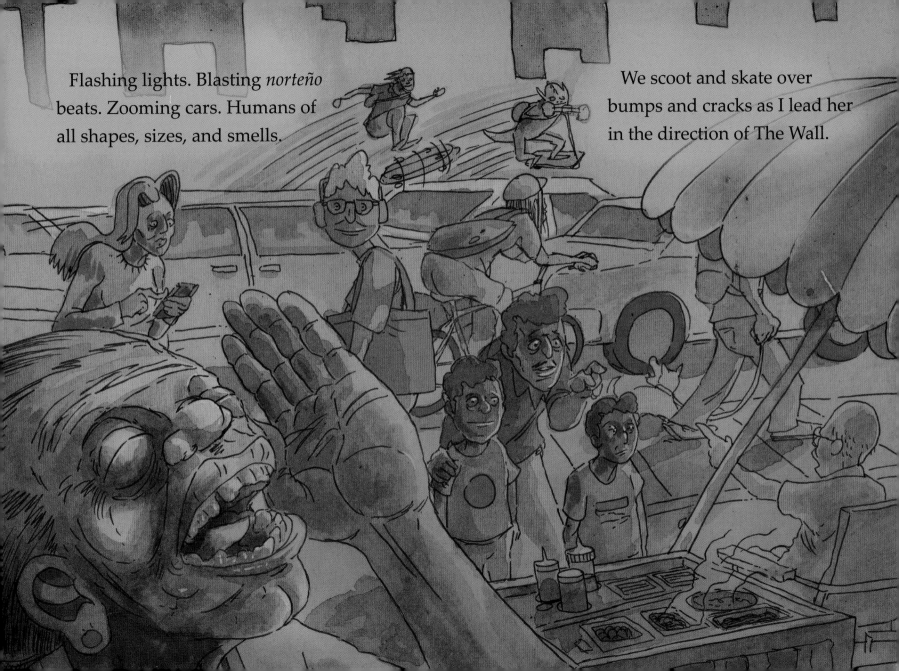

Flashing lights. Blasting *norteño* beats. Zooming cars. Humans of all shapes, sizes, and smells.

We scoot and skate over bumps and cracks as I lead her in the direction of The Wall.

Sidewalks stop and dirt begins.
Coyotes howl their ancient sounds to
the shining full moon.
    As we inch up to The Wall, we twirl
around a swirl of people curled up
asleep in the shadow of The Wall.

We want adventure, so we agree. We must climb. We try our best, grabbing metal edges, but we slip over and over again. We fall to the ground, exhausted. Dang it! ¡Qué lástima!

Lying in a dustheap at the feet of The Wall we hear the cries of *niños* lost and never found.

We hear a rumble and then a murmur. The Wall is speaking to us!

"They need your help, Lupe and Charlie. Follow the coyote. She will lead you to a tunnel. Tell the snake who guards it that The Wall sent you."

"Then what?" we ask The Wall.

"The tunnel leads to *el otro lado*—the other side of The Wall. Here you'll follow the dried out river till you find *El Señor Paletero Man*. He has *la llave de plata*—the silver key. You'll know what to do once you have it. But beware of the Big People in Green. Like dragons, they will shoot fire and smoke at you."

We can't believe our luck. We're going on a real adventure.

So, Lupe and I do as we are told. We follow the coyote. We meet the snake. She grants safe passage to el otro lado and shows us the tunnel we must crawl through.

We crawl on our elbows and knees for a long time until the
tunnel spits us out on the other side of The Wall. Under the bright
moonlight, we find the path of the dried out river. We find El
Señor Paletero Man with la llave de plata.

"Lupe and Charlie, I've been waiting for you. You must take this
key and free the niños. The Big People in Green keep them locked
in cages *allá*!"

We creep around to the other side of a big rock, and we spot the Big People in Green. They spot us too. Flashing lights. *Ladridos.* Gnashing teeth.

We see the cages, and we run to them. Lickety-split, with la llave de plata, Lupe click-clicks the key in the locks, opening them all.

The niños all shout, "¡*Corran!*
¡*Corran!* ¡*Corran!*" Scattering in all
directions, we all escape. Lupe and
I run for The Wall.

But we can't find the snake
or the coyote or the tunnel.
"How will we get home?"
Lupe asks me.

We're cold and tired, so we sit on the ground.

We have to be home before morning. Before our parents notice we're gone.

"We need to find El Señor Paletero Man," I tell Lupe.

We walk quickly, retracing our steps from earlier in the night, and we find El Señor Paletero Man.

"We freed the niños, but we need to get home before sunrise, El Señor Paletero Man," I tell him.

"With so little time, the only *manera* is to fly," he says.

"But you're in luck. My friend *El Señor Big Bigote* has the biggest mustache in the land. He can whisk you back to your *familias* in the nick of time. The path of the three-prickly-pear cactus will lead you to him."

Hurrying down the path of the three-prickly-pear cactus, we find El Señor Big Bigote with his head tucked under the hood of a '67 Chevy Impala.

"El Señor Big Bigote, would you fly us across The Wall so we can be home before dawn?" we beg him. And then we offer him the giant jar of pickles.

"With such a gift how can I refuse? And I want to try out my latest pickle-powered combustion engine. Let's go, niños." With seatbelts fastened and windows down, El Señor Big Bigote zips us through the sky.

We search down below us for
my cuarto de azotea in the sky.
Finally, we see it!
We land and Lupe disappears
over the roof's edge.
I slip into bed, smiling big.
I know this will be the first of
many great adventures.

LEGEND OF EL CHUPACABRA

Latinxs have lots of tales with monsters, some real and some imagined. Be careful when you are around a river or lake, as the wailing, distraught La Llorona has been known to drown children. If you misbehave, the ghost monster El Cucuy will come and eat you up. And if you find yourself in the cornfields, woods, or ravines across the Southwest and Puerto Rico, beware of the blood-sucking, hairless mutts with big claws and the spikey-backed chupacabras lurking there.

The author and illustrator of this book have first-hand experience with El Chupacabra. Near where Chris Escobar grew up in Santa Barbara, he'd hear chupacabra shrieks and coyote howls at night, coming from the nearby ravine. And in the rural northern California area where Frederick "Fede" Aldama grew up, chickens went missing, leaving behind only feathers and flesh in their coop—and he knew it was the work of El Chupacabra.

To this day, Chris and Fede keep eyes and ears wide open for signs of El Chupacabra.

GLOSSARY

allá	over there
animalitos	little animals
atúnes	tunas
¿Cómo te llamas?	What is your name?
corran	run
cosas	things
cuarto de azotea	breeze-block room that sits atop flat roofs in Mexico
desayuno	breakfast
el otro lado	the other side, and usually used in the context of crossing the US/Mexico border
El Señor Big Bigote	man with a big mustache (*bigote* means "mustache")
El Señor Paletero Man	man who pushes a cart down the streets, selling ice cream, shaved ice, and Mexican ice-pops
Estados Unidos	United States of America
familias	families
Jumex	brand of juice and nectar popular in Mexico and with Latinxs in the US
la llave de plata	the silver key
ladridos	barking
libros	books
manera	way
niños	children
norteña	a type of music that originated in the nineteenth century in northern Mexico and around the US/Mexico border; the musicians use accordions and 12-string guitars while singing mostly ballads
primos	cousins
¡Qué lástima!	What a shame!
tortugas	turtles